For my little girl Lucy

A special thank-you to Zoe Krosoczka
for the art assist on this book

THIS IS A BORZOI BOOK PUBLISHED BY ALFRED A. KNOPF

Copyright © 2014 by Jarrett J. Krosoczka

All rights reserved. Published in the United States by Alfred A. Knopf, an imprint of
Random House Children's Books, a division of Random House, Inc., New York.

Knopf, Borzoi Books, and the colophon are registered trademarks of Random House, Inc.

Visit us on the Web! randomhouse.com/kids

Educators and librarians, for a variety of teaching tools, visit us at RHTeachersLibrarians.com

Library of Congress Cataloging-in-Publication Data
Krosoczka, Jarrett.
Peanut Butter and Jellyfish / Jarrett J. Krosoczka. — First edition.
p.   cm.
Summary: "Best friends Peanut Butter and Jellyfish are constantly being taunted by
their neighbor, Crabby, until they help him out of a jam."—Provided by publisher
ISBN 978-0-375-87036-1 (trade) — ISBN 978-0-375-97036-8 (lib. bdg.) — ISBN 978-0-307-97967-4 (ebook)
[1. Bullies—Fiction. 2. Sea horses—Fiction. 3. Jellyfishes—Fiction.
4. Crabs—Fiction. 5. Friendship—Fiction.] I. Title.
PZ7.K935Pe 2014
[E]—dc23
2013003155

The text of this book is set in 18-point Bokka Solid.
The illustrations were created using digital collage of acrylic paintings.

MANUFACTURED IN CHINA

April 2014
10 9 8 7 6 5 4 3
First Edition

Jarrett J. Krosoczka

Peanut Butter and Jellyfish

ALFRED A. KNOPF
NEW YORK

Peanut Butter and Jellyfish were
the best of friends.

Best of friends who spent their days exploring

up,

down.

around,

and through their grand ocean home.

unluckily for them, though,
they lived near Crabby.

"You guys swim like humans!"
he would taunt as they slipped past.

Peanut Butter and Jellyfish did
their best to ignore the heckler.

Crabby was relentless.

"You guys smell like rotten barnacles! Pee-yew!"

"My grandma called. She wants her run-walk shoes back!"

Jellyfish puffed up his chest and said, "Driftwood and sea stones may break our bones, but words will never hurt us."

"You're an invertebrate! You don't even *have* any bones," huffed Crabby as he marched along his favorite rock by himself.

One day, as Peanut Butter and Jellyfish set out on an excursion to the great reef, they swam past Crabby's perch. They braced themselves for the usual insults. But all was quiet.

Then they heard the faint
sound of sobbing up ahead.

It was Crabby! He was caught in a
lobster trap. And it was being lifted
to the surface!

"I'm scared,"
he cried.

Surely, he was doomed.

"Should we help?" asked Jellyfish.
The two friends shared a look.

"He *is* in serious trouble," said
Peanut Butter.

"You're right. We *have* to help!"
exclaimed Jellyfish. "But how?"

"I have a plan," said
Peanut Butter. "Follow me."

They swam up to the lobster trap.

Peanut Butter used his tail to
unlock the trap's gate, but Crabby
didn't budge.

"Come on. You're free!" said Peanut
Butter.

"But—but . . . I can't swim,"
confessed Crabby. "And I'm afraid of
heights."

The lobster trap was getting pulled
closer to the surface!

"Plan B!" exclaimed Jellyfish. He worked furiously on untying the trap's knot.

"Hurry!" cried Peanut Butter. "I can see the fishermen above!"

Just when all hope was lost . . .

The knot gave out, sending the trap plummeting! Peanut Butter and Jellyfish grabbed ahold and lowered it to safety.

Crabby's legs wobbled as he returned to his favorite rock. "Th-thanks, you t-two," he stuttered.

"You know, I'm sorry for saying those mean things," Crabby said. He may have been afraid of heights, but Crabby was brave enough to apologize.

"I guess I was jealous. You guys seem like you're always having so much fun exploring the open waters."

"Well, there's plenty to explore close to the ocean floor!" said Jellyfish.

Peanut Butter and Jellyfish still swam up, down, around, and through. But it was on the ocean floor that they found their greatest treasure!